This is a work of fiction. Names, characters, places, and incidents are either the product of the author's imagination or used fictitiously.

Published by Sukhpreet Singh

For permissions, contact:
baapdaada13@gmail.com

ISBN: 978-93-343-1514-1

Cover and Interior Design by Sukhpreet Singh

To the soul covered in dust, not damage —
the light was always yours.

NOT BROKEN, JUST BURIED

Sukhpreet Singh

Published by Sukhpreet Singh

CONTENTS

CHAPTER 1 – THE MOVE

"Sometimes a fresh start is just a new place to carry the same pain."

The moving truck pulled away just before sunset, leaving behind a trail of dust, a broken flowerpot, and my doubt.

Arjun stood beside me, hands on his hips, his eyes fixed on the small, two-story house at the end of the cul-de-sac. It was quiet here. A kind of quiet that felt too still, like a photograph.

"Looks better without the previous owner's junk, right?" he said, trying to sound optimistic. I nodded, but didn't answer. My arms were tired, not from the boxes — but from months of holding everything in.

Ira tugged at my kurta. "Mumma, can I pick my room now?"

I smiled. "Of course, baby. Go find the sunniest one."

She ran inside, barefoot, her giggle echoing through the empty hallway like it didn't know yet what had happened to us.

#

We moved here for peace. Or maybe we moved because we were running out of things to pretend.

The old apartment was loud, yes — but it wasn't the traffic. It was the way we stopped talking. The way Arjun started staying late at work. The way I started sleeping facing the other side of the bed.

This house was supposed to fix us. A fresh chapter. A hopeful line between “before” and “after.”

But the truth was, I already felt something strange here. Not haunted, not scary. Just… like the house was listening.

#

The door creaked open again behind me. Arjun walked in, brushing his hands.

“Neighbors seem nice,” he said. “Lady next door brought tea earlier. Suzette or something. She seemed—friendly.”

I didn’t reply. I was staring at the walls.

They had repainted everything before selling. Off-white. Safe. But not new.

I could still see faint patches where old photo frames had once hung — small rectangles where memories used to live.

This wasn’t a clean slate. This was a house with a wiped face.

#

I started unpacking the kitchen first. Something about cups and plates always made me feel grounded. A home with washed dishes always felt alive.

Ira was upstairs. Arjun was on the phone. I didn’t ask who it was.

Then there was a knock.

#

A woman stood at the door — tall, around fifty, with a simple cotton sari and tired, observant eyes. She had a steel tiffin in her hand.

“You’re the new madam?” she asked.

I nodded. “Yes. Just moved in today.”

“I’m Meera. I used to help the previous lady who lived here. She left in a hurry. Said she didn’t want to come back. I clean. I cook. If you need help, I live two lanes away.”

There was something about her tone. No emotion. Just fact.

“What happened to her?”

Meera’s eyes flickered. “Some people leave places. Some leave themselves behind."

Before I could reply, she added, "Do you want me to start tomorrow?"

I hesitated. But something about her presence — calm, still — made me say, "Yes."

#

That night, as I lay beside Arjun, his back turned to mine, I stared at the ceiling fan spinning above us. It creaked. Just a little.

Like something was unsettled.

Ira's soft breathing from the next room was my only anchor.

I thought moving would make me feel lighter. But it was here, in this new house, that I realized how heavy silence can be.

#

In the middle of the night, I woke up to find Arjun gone. His pillow was cold.

I found him downstairs, standing by the window. His phone in his hand, screen still lit.

He didn't notice me. Or maybe he did, and chose not to.

I went back to bed.

#

As I closed my eyes again, I remembered something Meera said.
"Some people leave themselves behind."

Maybe she wasn't talking about the last owner.
Maybe she was talking about me

The next morning smelled like dust and lemon cleaner.

Ira burst into the kitchen, holding something in her hands — a folded paper with jagged edges.

"Look what I found in the floor vent!" she said. "It was stuck!"

I dried my hands and took it from her. It was part of a letter, yellowed, like it had been there for years. The handwriting was rushed, messy — more like someone escaping thoughts than writing them down.

"...I hear them even when I know they aren't real. Sometimes the silence isn't silence at all. It's just something hiding beneath it..."

There was no name. No date.

Just the words. Hanging. Cold.

Ira tugged my arm. "What does it mean, Mumma?"

I forced a smile. "Just someone's old note. Maybe they were writing a story."

She nodded, satisfied, and skipped off.

But my hands were still holding the paper too tightly.

#

Later that day, while unpacking bedroom boxes, I found a cracked photo frame tucked behind a drawer. A woman — mid-30s, sharp cheekbones, tired eyes — stood smiling with a man and a small boy. Same wall. Same window. Same house.

But the photo was split right down the middle, like someone had dropped it. Or thrown it.

I didn't recognize them, but somehow, I felt them.

#

At night, the house changed.

In daylight, it was old but warm. At night, it grew quiet in a different way — like the walls had breath, and they were holding it in.

Arjun was asleep. Or pretending to bc.

I walked barefoot to the kitchen for water.

The hallway creaked.

A cupboard door was ajar — though I was sure I had closed everything. Small things, unexplainable. But too small to call strange.

#

When I returned to bed, I stared at the ceiling again. This time, no fan.

Just thought.

#

"What if places remember?"
"What if pain leaves footprints even where people don't?"

#

I heard a light knock on Ira's door and froze.
One soft tap.

I held my breath. Waited.

Nothing else.

I walked slowly to her room and opened it — she was asleep, curled into her blanket, the paper she'd found still beside her pillow.

I picked it up.

Looked at it again under the dim lamp.

One word I hadn't noticed before, faint in the top corner, barely inked.

"Meera."

I stared at it.

And for the first time since we moved in, I wasn't sure this was going to be a new beginning.

CHAPTER 2 – THE MAID

"Some people speak in words. Others speak in presence."

Meera arrived at exactly nine.

No doorbell. Just a soft knock — two taps, and then stillness.

I opened the door. She nodded once, stepped in, and walked straight to the kitchen like she already knew the way.

She wore the same pale green sari, neatly pleated, with her hair tied in a bun that didn't move when she did. Her hands moved quickly, efficiently — washing, wiping, aligning. Not one question asked. Not one word wasted.

It was unsettling how familiar she felt in a house that wasn't even mine yet.

#

I followed her quietly, pretending to look for something in the cupboard.

"So... you worked for the family before us?" I asked, casually.

She didn't stop. "Yes. For six months."

"Why did they leave?"

She paused. Just a moment. Then said, "Some people leave when it gets too loud. Even if no one else hears the noise."

I didn't know what to say to that. She didn't look at me when she said it — her focus was still on scrubbing the sink like it had offended her.

I changed the subject.

#

After Arjun left for work, I took my coffee to the front porch. The sun was warm but soft, and Ira was inside drawing — something about the way she colored trees made me think she remembered a life more peaceful than mine.

Meera appeared by the side gate an hour later, holding something small in her hand.

"Found this buried in the soil by the garden tiles," she said. "Looked personal."

It was a torn photograph — bent, stained, edges curling. A boy, maybe five or six, holding a paper plane, smiling wide. I looked closer.

Same boy from the frame I'd found yesterday. This time without the parents.

Ira called from inside. "Mumma, where's the glitter glue?"

Meera's eyes were still on me.

I took the photo. "Thank you."

She nodded and walked back to sweeping the porch. Silent again.

#

There was something about her. Not just quiet — **still**. She didn't try to belong, but she didn't feel separate either. She wasn't part of the house, yet she fit like she had always been here. Like dust in corners that never really leaves.

#

That evening, I started writing.

I hadn't written in months — not since things with Arjun began to stretch thinner than silence.

The journal was new, a gift I gave myself when we decided to move. I opened to the first page and wrote one sentence:

"I don't think the house is haunted. I think I am."

#

Arjun came home late. Again.

He smelled like sweat and deodorant and traffic. He tossed his bag on the chair and sank onto the sofa without looking at me.

"Clients were annoying. My head is spinning," he said, rubbing his eyes.

I asked if he ate anything. He didn't reply.

We sat in the same room for ten minutes without speaking. I went back to my journal.

He glanced at it. "Still doing that?"

I looked up. "Doing what?"

"That self-help thing. Writing stuff down like it's gonna change anything."

I closed the book slowly. "Maybe it won't. But maybe I will."

He blinked at me. That was all. No reply.

#

Later that night, after Ira slept and the house returned to its usual hum of refrigerator motors and creaking wood, I found Meera still in the kitchen. Her sari had traces of turmeric and steam. She was wiping the stove slowly, almost rhythmically.

"You don't have to stay this late," I said.

She looked up. Her eyes were deep — not in color, but in the kind of quiet that makes you nervous.

"I don't watch the clock," she said. "I stop when the house feels... lighter."

I wasn't sure what that meant. But part of me understood.

#

"You said something this morning," I said. "About people hearing noise even if no one else does."

Meera wiped her hands, folded the cloth carefully.

"Everyone carries something they don't name," she replied. "Sometimes it echoes."

I walked to the window, stared out at the neighbor's porch. Empty.

"What happened to the woman who lived here before me?" I asked. "The one you worked for."

"She smiled a lot," Meera said. "But her eyes were too tired to hold it."

"Did she leave alone?"

Pause.

"No one really leaves alone."

#

She packed her tiffin, nodded to me like a closing ritual, and left through the side door.

As soon as she was gone, the room felt heavier. Not darker —just like something had gone missing that wasn't fully visible to begin with.

#

I checked on Ira. Her glitter glue project was now a collage of sky and trees and stars. She'd cut out paper people and glued them beneath the stars.

One was labeled "Mumma."

One "Me."

And one — "The Quiet One."

I pointed. "Who's that?"

She shrugged. "The maid. She doesn't talk, but I like her. She doesn't make noise in my head."

#

That night, before sleeping, I stood at the kitchen sink and looked out the small window. Across the backyard, the trees moved gently in the breeze.

And then I saw it.

A figure.

Standing by the fence, half-shadowed.

Not moving. Just standing.

I blinked.

Gone.

Nothing.

Maybe a trick of light. Maybe something else.

#

In bed, I asked Arjun, "Do you feel anything different here?"

He grunted. "It's a house. Walls. Doors. What's to feel?"

I turned to face the ceiling.

"Maybe I'm not just looking for peace," I whispered. "Maybe I'm

waiting for something to remember me."

#

The next morning, I woke up with a sentence in my mind — like a dream that left behind a fingerprint:

"This house doesn't need fixing. It needs forgiving."

And when I came downstairs, Meera was already there.

Wiping the same spot on the counter. As if she'd never left.

The next afternoon, I found Meera standing still in the hallway — not working, just looking at the wall opposite the staircase.

I paused behind her. "Is something wrong?"

She didn't answer right away. Then, without turning, she said, "This wall used to have mirrors."

"Mirrors?"

She nodded. "A full set. Long ones. The woman who lived here before — she said she needed to remember who she was."

"And did she?"

"No," Meera said, finally turning. "She broke them all."

I looked at the wall — bare, smooth now. No signs. But I imagined the shatter, the glass flying, the moment someone couldn't face their own reflection anymore.

I knew that feeling too well.

#

That night, I couldn't sleep.

There was no sound, no light, no distraction. Just the low hum of thought — the kind that doesn't whisper, but circles.

I opened my journal again and wrote:

"There is a woman in this house I do not know. She left. But she didn't take her pain with her."

I closed the journal and went downstairs to get water.

And that's when I saw the kitchen drawer — the one beneath the sink — slightly open.

I hadn't touched it all day.

I stepped closer and pulled it gently.

Inside: a single piece of paper, folded into a square.

It wasn't there before. I was sure.

I opened it. The ink was faded, but readable:

"I tried everything. Silence. Screaming. Smiling. But this house doesn't forget. And neither do I."

No name. No date. Just the ache of someone who once tried to survive.

#

The next day, I asked Meera directly.

"Did something happen here?"

Her hands didn't stop peeling garlic. She said, "Something always happens. In every house."

I pressed. "But here. This family. The woman."

She didn't look up. "She kept asking for peace, but every day she fed her pain. Peace doesn't come when you hold hands with the past."

I leaned against the counter. "Did she leave because of him? The husband?"

This time Meera stopped.

"She left because she forgot who she was. He just helped her forget faster."

The words hit harder than I expected. Maybe because they felt too close to my own story.

#

That evening, Ira showed me her new drawing.

A tree with no leaves.

Only roots.

"They're not dead," she said. "They're just sleeping underneath."

I didn't know if she was talking about the tree or me.

#

Later that night, I stood in the hallway and touched the smooth wall where the mirrors once were.

I imagined placing one again. Looking at myself fully.

Not the mother. Not the wife. Not the tired eyes or polite voice.

Just the girl beneath it all. The one who used to write poetry in her college notebook. The one who wanted stillness before the world gave her noise.

#

Meera was at the door the next morning when I opened it — same time, same sari, same quiet.

But this time she brought a small packet of jasmine flowers and placed them in a bowl on the dining table.

"For fragrance?" I asked.

"For energy," she said. "This house needs softness."

I didn't ask how she knew. Somehow, I believed her.

#

By the time she left that evening, the house felt... not lighter exactly, but warmer.

I stood in the doorway after she left, holding the edges of my shawl, watching her disappear down the lane.

Just before she turned the corner, she paused.

And without looking back, she said loud enough for me to hear:

"Forgiveness is not something you give to them.
It's what you stop taking from yourself."

Then she walked on.

#

And in that moment, I felt something I hadn't felt in months.

Not peace.

But the faint memory of it.

Like a room I once lived in. Locked. Waiting.

CHAPTER 3 – THE CRACKS

"Most people don't shatter all at once. They fracture, slowly, where no one looks."

It began with the receipts.

Two of them. Folded, crumpled, buried in Arjun's jacket pocket while I was hanging it after dinner. Not hidden well — just lazy enough to make me doubt whether I was supposed to find them or not.

One was from a restaurant we'd never visited together.

The other from a petrol pump 40 minutes away — the same evening he told me he worked late.

I stared at the thin paper for a long time. Not with anger. Just quiet.

Like someone listening to a familiar song that now sounded off-key.

#

The next morning, I placed both slips on the side table, beside his keys.

He didn't mention them. Just pocketed the keys and said, "Don't wait for me tonight. Might be another long one."

I smiled. A reflex more than a response.

He left without looking back.

#

Meera arrived ten minutes later, as always — carrying a small jar of homemade pickles and a look that could cut through steel.

She noticed the half-empty teacup near the sink and asked nothing. That's how she was — no curiosity, but full awareness.

"I cleaned upstairs yesterday," she said. "Today I'll do the storeroom."

"There's a storeroom?" I asked.

She nodded. "Back of the kitchen. Hidden behind that tall shelf."

I followed her.

#

It was a narrow space, low-ceilinged, with uneven walls and a faint scent of old paper and wood polish. Boxes were stacked along one side, a broken fan on the other.

On the wall — scribbled in black ink, almost lost in dust — a line:

"You forget who you are when you start counting how many times you've been wrong."

I stared at it. My throat tightened.

Meera just brushed past it like it wasn't there. But I caught the flicker in her eyes.

"You knew that was here?" I asked.

"I know what most people avoid," she said.

I didn't reply.

#

That night, Ira asked me if daddies always stay the same.

"What do you mean?" I asked.

"I mean... do they always smile when they come home? Or do they change sometimes?"

I swallowed slowly. "They don't mean to change. Life gets heavy. Sometimes they forget how to be light."

She looked at me. "You don't forget. You're always soft."

I wanted to tell her that wasn't true. That some nights I curled up like a question with no answer.

But I didn't.

Because she needed me to be the soft one.

#

Meera stayed later that evening. Said she was "finishing something."

She cleaned the glass cabinet in the dining room. Then, without asking, rearranged the books on the bottom shelf. As she did, a small diary fell out.

Thin, dark cover. No name.

I picked it up.

On the inside flap — a single name scribbled faintly.

"Aisha."

I didn't recognize it.

But I knew instinctively: she was the woman who lived here before me.

#

That night, I opened the diary.

The first few pages were torn.

The middle pages had writing — fast, anxious, sometimes crossing over itself like the writer couldn't keep up with her own thoughts.

"I kept waiting for him to see me again. The way he used to — like I was light.
But the more I tried to be perfect, the more invisible I became."

"I stopped arguing, thinking that would bring peace. But silence is only golden when it's shared."

I felt my chest tighten — not with jealousy, but recognition.

These weren't just her words.
They were mine too. Written by a different hand.

"Sometimes the person who hurts you most is the one you once prayed for."

The diary haunted me.

Not because it was dramatic — but because it wasn't. It wasn't filled with rage. It was filled with small, quiet heartbreaks.

Aisha hadn't left because something big happened.

She left because **nothing did.**

#

The next morning, I watched Arjun while he buttered his toast.

He didn't notice me watching.

He scrolled through his phone. Smiled once. Quickly.

Then caught me staring.

"What?"

"Who's Aisha?"

He blinked. His fingers paused over the toast.

"The woman who lived here," I added.

"I don't know," he said too fast. "Why?"

I shrugged. "Just found something she left behind."

Arjun looked back at his phone. "Weird. Probably a sad woman. These houses always come with some baggage."

I wanted to ask why he seemed so familiar with that kind of baggage.

But I didn't.

Because part of me didn't want to know the answer.

#

After he left, I placed the diary back where I found it. Not to forget it — but to let it breathe.

I sat on the floor near the window. Light poured in like memory.

And I wrote in my own journal:

"The cracks in my marriage are not loud. They are polite. They sip coffee with me. Sleep beside me. Carry bags into new homes."

#

That evening, Meera made tea.

She handed me a cup without asking if I wanted one. She always knew.

I asked her, "Do you believe people can change?"

She stirred sugar into her own cup — two spoons, no clink of the spoon, just a gentle swirl.

"Change?" she repeated.

"Yes. Like really change. Come back from being cold. Become good again."

She looked at me — really looked.

"No one becomes cold for no reason," she said. "But some

people stay cold because it becomes easier than healing."

"And can they heal?"

"Yes. But only when losing the cold feels safer than keeping it."

#

After she left, I called Arjun.

He picked up after three rings.

"Where are you?" I asked.

"Work," he said.

I could hear wind behind him.

"I made your favorite for dinner."

Pause.

"I'll be late."

"Who were you texting during breakfast?"

"Sanjana—"

"I'm not accusing. I'm asking."

He sighed. "Don't start. I'm already tired."

He hung up.

#

I sat there, phone still warm in my hand, staring at the wallpaper. There was a tiny bubble near the corner where it peeled. Something about it annoyed me more than it should've.

That's the thing with cracks.

They start where you least expect them.

#

That night, I opened the attic door.

It was dusty, unused. The bulb flickered like it had forgotten how to stay lit.

Boxes. Old sheets. A cracked mirror propped against the side.

I picked up a file folder near the back.

Inside were utility bills. Old photographs.

And a birth certificate.

Aisha Roy. Age: 34. Spouse: Rohan Roy.

The name wasn't familiar. But the signature below was.

Arjun Singh.

Witness signature.
I stared.
And suddenly the cracks weren't small anymore.

#

I took the file downstairs, laid it on the dining table.
Ira was asleep.
Meera had already left.
I stared at the signature again.
He had known her.
Not just known — he'd witnessed her marriage.
In this house.
Years before me.

#

I called him again.
He didn't pick up.
I didn't call again.

#

I went to the kitchen and poured water slowly.
Glass. Cold. Shaking just slightly.
And then I whispered to no one:
"Maybe the ghost here isn't her.
Maybe it's who I used to be."

CHAPTER 4 – THE UNSEEN MIRROR

"Sometimes the scariest thing isn't what's hiding in the dark — it's what's hiding in plain sight."

I didn't ask Arjun about the signature the next day.

I watched him instead.

The way he avoided eye contact. The way he rushed out after breakfast. The way he didn't kiss Ira goodbye.

People don't just lie with words.

They lie with timing. With the silence between simple things.

#

Meera noticed the file before I even mentioned it.

She saw it on the corner of the table while wiping around it.

"You found something," she said.

I nodded. "Did you know Arjun was connected to the woman who lived here before me?"

She didn't act surprised.

"Some connections are not meant to last. Only to teach."

"That's a very polite way of saying he's hiding something."

She kept wiping, slow, deliberate. "Pain doesn't always come from betrayal. Sometimes it comes from seeing someone choose the same darkness — again."

I sat down, suddenly exhausted.

"You think I should confront him?"

"I think," Meera said, "you already have. Just not with words yet."

#

Later that day, while folding laundry in Ira's room, I noticed something taped under her pillow.

A note. Childish handwriting.

"When Mumma cries, I feel it in my chest. But she thinks I don't know."

I sat on her bed and didn't move for five minutes.

Just held the paper.

Like it was proof that pain echoes louder through silence than sound.

#

That evening, the mirror in the guest bathroom cracked.

No one touched it.

No one even used that room.

A long, thin line — straight down the middle — like a seam splitting open.

I ran my fingers along the crack.

Meera appeared behind me in the hallway.

"Glass doesn't break alone," she said. "Something moves beneath it first."

#

At dinner, Arjun scrolled through his phone again.

This time, I didn't pretend not to notice.

"You signed Aisha's marriage certificate," I said.

He froze. Just for a moment. Then resumed chewing.

"Yes."

"That's all?"

"We were friends. Briefly. Before I met you."

"You never mentioned it."

"Because it didn't matter. It was years ago."

"She lived here. You knew that."

He looked at me now. "What are you suggesting?"

I shook my head. "Nothing. Just wondering why so many

ghosts live rent-free between us."

He scoffed. "This again? You've always had a flair for drama."

I stood up.

"No. I just stopped pretending broken glass is sunlight."

#

That night, I lay in bed alone. Arjun on the couch.

I stared at the ceiling and wrote in my journal:

"You can't rebuild trust over cracks. You have to tear it down to the foundation."

#

In the quiet, I heard the faintest click.

Not a door. Not a drawer.

A mirror.

Somewhere in the house, something had shifted again.

And it wasn't just the glass.

"The reflection doesn't lie. It just waits for you to stop pretending."

The next morning, I avoided Arjun. Not out of anger — but self-preservation.

I made breakfast for Ira, packed her schoolbag, and kissed her forehead the way I always do. She smiled, but something in her eyes felt older than it should have.

Meera came in as I was staring at the cracked mirror again.

"You're not really looking at yourself," she said softly. "You're looking for who you lost."

I turned toward her. "And if that person doesn't want to come back?"

"Then ask," she said, "why you ever left her behind."

#

The house was unusually quiet that day.

No street noise. No birds. Even Ira's glitter drawings lay untouched on the table.

I spent most of the morning cleaning, then pretending I wasn't cleaning just to stay busy.

At noon, I stood near the window, and suddenly — I

remembered something.

An old version of me.

In college. Standing in front of an open mic, shaking, reading a poem about fear and love in the same breath.

That girl wasn't gone.

She was just buried beneath the woman who learned to apologize before being blamed.

#

Meera brought me a cup of ginger tea and sat beside me for the first time.

She never sat.

It felt sacred, almost.

I asked her, "Do you ever wonder what would've happened if you made different choices?"

She smiled faintly. "I don't wonder. I remember."

I frowned. "What do you mean?"

"Some of us carry memory that's older than our names," she said. "We don't need to imagine another life. We just need to listen to the echoes inside this one."

I didn't fully understand — but part of me did.

Somewhere deep, beyond logic.

#

Later that evening, I went to the attic again.

Same bulb. Same boxes. But something was different.

There was a small, framed quote now sitting on the floor where I'd left nothing:

"The soul always knows when it's being ignored."

I picked it up, heart pounding.

Was it Aisha's?

Or had it always been here?

Or was the house... remembering?

#

That night, Arjun came home late again.

Smelled like perfume. His shirt collar had a faint smudge. Lipstick? Or guilt?

I didn't ask.

Instead, I said, "I think we need to talk."

He sighed, dropped his bag.

"You always want to talk when I want to forget."

I stepped closer.

"No. I always stay quiet when I should speak."

He stared at me — surprised.

I pointed to the cracked mirror behind him. "That's how we look now. Together, but split. Don't you feel it?"

"I'm tired," he said.

"So am I. But I'm also awake."

#

That night, I couldn't sleep. So I walked to the guest bathroom and stood before the cracked glass.

I looked into my own eyes for a long time.

And I said out loud — not to anyone, but to the version of me behind the surface:

"You're not broken. You're just buried.
And I'm coming to find you."

#

In the silence, I heard Meera humming downstairs.

A low, ancient tune. One that didn't belong to now.

And in that moment, I knew:

She wasn't just a maid.

She was someone sent to **watch the soul, not the house.**

CHAPTER 5 – THE VISITOR

"Some visitors bring questions. Others bring mirrors."

It was a Tuesday when she showed up.

Ira was coloring in the living room, the TV was murmuring in the background, and I was folding laundry that no one thanked me for.

The doorbell rang at 4:16 p.m.

I opened it expecting a delivery.

Instead, I saw a woman — maybe in her late thirties, holding a blue tote bag and a phone like she'd just checked my address three times.

"Is this 14, Devika Lane?" she asked.

"Yes."

She nodded, breathed in, and said, "I used to live here."

I froze.

"You're Aisha?"

She blinked. "No. My name is **Rhea.** I'm her sister."

#

She stepped inside slowly, her eyes scanning the hallway like they were tracing ghosts.

"I'm sorry to drop in. I just... I wasn't sure I'd do this, but I was in town and thought I'd see it one last time."

Her voice had the kind of ache that comes from holding in too much for too long.

I offered tea. She refused. Just water.

Meera came out from the kitchen quietly, gave a short nod to Rhea, and disappeared again — like she'd known she was coming.

#

"She didn't leave any of her things," Rhea said, looking around. "But I still feel her here."

I sat across from her. "I found a diary. And a photo. And... your sister's name."

Rhea swallowed. "Did Arjun tell you they knew each other?"

I didn't answer.

She nodded anyway. "He was there in the beginning. Helped them get this house. But things went dark. She stopped telling me everything."

I watched her hands — fidgeting, then still.

"She called me one night, crying. Said the house wasn't letting her breathe. That she kept forgetting who she was. And then, a week later, she left."

I leaned forward. "Left him?"

"She left everything."

#

There was a pause — a heavy one.

Rhea looked me in the eye. "Are you okay living here?"

It was a question with too many layers.

I didn't lie. "Some days I forget how to be."

She gave a half-smile. "Then maybe this house isn't cursed. Maybe it just reveals what we try to hide."

#

Before she left, she handed me a key.

"I found this in her things. It was labeled 'Attic Drawer.' I never knew what it opened. But I kept it."

I took it, small and rusted.

Rhea placed her hand briefly over mine.

"She wasn't crazy," she whispered. "Just too sensitive for a world that rewards silence over truth."

And then she was gone.

#

I sat alone for an hour, the key still in my hand.

I didn't open the attic yet.

Not because I was afraid of what I'd find.

But because I was afraid it might reflect too clearly what I already knew.

#

That night, I told Arjun that Rhea had come.

He looked surprised. Then annoyed.

"She had no right. This is our house now."

"Maybe not. Maybe it's just where we keep living out other people's lies."

He walked away.

Didn't argue.

Didn't explain.

And I didn't chase him.

Because this time, I knew the silence wasn't mine to fix.

"Truth doesn't always scream. Sometimes it waits in a drawer you're too scared to open."

That night, after Arjun fell asleep on the couch again, I climbed the attic stairs with the small rusted key clenched in my fist.

The house creaked with each step like it was breathing heavier the closer I got.

Dust hung in the air like it hadn't moved in years.

I reached the wooden drawer tucked behind a stack of books and unopened boxes. There was no handle — just a faint groove.

I slid the key in.

It turned with a slow, tired click.

#

Inside: a bundle wrapped in cloth.

I unwrapped it, gently.

There were three things.

A small journal. A single earring — silver, shaped like a leaf.

And a folded letter addressed simply: *To whoever is next.*

My hands trembled.

I opened the letter first.

#

"If you're reading this, it means you feel it too. The weight. The air that pushes back.
This house doesn't haunt with ghosts. It haunts with memory.
I loved someone who stopped seeing me. And then I stopped seeing myself."

"I hope you're stronger. I hope you don't wait for the silence to eat you."

No name. No goodbye.

Just the kind of pain that doesn't beg — only leaves.

#

I sat there, on the cold attic floor, letter in my lap, the silver earring shining faintly like it remembered better light.

For the first time in weeks, I didn't feel scared.

I felt seen.

#

When I came downstairs, Meera was waiting.

She was never there that late. But she was standing by the kitchen table, as if she'd known exactly when I'd return.

"You found it," she said.

I didn't ask how she knew.

"Why didn't you tell me?" I asked.

"Because some truths need to be held, not handed. You had to choose to open it."

I looked at her — really looked.

"You're not just a maid, are you?"

She gave a faint smile. "No. But I clean. Just not furniture."

I swallowed. "Then what do you clean?"

She looked up — into my eyes, not past them.

"Dust.
From souls.
When they forget their shine."

#

I didn't cry. Not then.

Because it wasn't sadness anymore.

It was remembering.

The feeling of being seen without makeup, without roles, without fear.

Just me.

Beneath everything I'd carried.

#

The next morning, I took the journal, the earring, and the letter — and placed them in a wooden box on the window ledge.

A space for her. For Aisha.

For all the women who left themselves behind.

#

Ira came and sat beside me.

"Can I ask something?" she said.

"Of course."

"Are you still sad?"

I thought for a long time.

"No," I said. "I'm just… softer now."

She nodded. "You feel like you again."

#

When Meera left that day, she didn't say goodbye.

She simply placed a fresh jasmine flower on the kitchen counter.

And whispered, not to me — but maybe to the house:

"She remembered."

CHAPTER 6 – THE SOFT REBELLION

"Not all revolutions are loud. Some begin when a woman finally chooses herself."

I woke up before sunrise.

The house was still. Even the shadows felt like they were resting.

I sat on the balcony, wrapped in a shawl, sipping tea I made for myself without asking who else wanted any.

It was the first morning in years I didn't start by checking on Arjun.

#

When he finally walked into the kitchen, rubbing his eyes, I didn't move.

He looked at me like I was doing something wrong just by being still.

"You're up early."

I nodded. "I slept well."

He raised an eyebrow. "Really?"

"Yes," I said. "For the first time in a long time. I wasn't waiting for you."

There was silence. The kind that usually ends in apology or anger.

But this time, it just... lingered.

#

Ira came in and hugged me without saying anything.

Arjun kissed the top of her head and left for work.

No goodbyes.

No lies this time either.

Just distance.

#

By 10 a.m., I had moved the furniture around in the living room.

Shifted the couch. Pulled down a painting I never liked. Opened every window.

Meera arrived and paused at the doorway like she was entering a temple.

"You've changed the air," she said, walking through with slow steps.

"I wanted space."

"For what?"

"To breathe without permission."

#

We cleaned together, side by side. No music. No talking for a while.

Then Meera handed me a stack of books she found behind the old cabinet.

One of them fell open.

A page was marked with a thin thread.

"You don't lose your voice all at once. You misplace it. In compromise. In silence. In shrinking to fit someone else's comfort."

I traced the words with my fingers.

"You think it's too late?" I asked.

"For what?"

"To change the way things are."

Meera didn't answer right away.

Then she said, "Even trees bend toward light when they've been growing in shadow too long."

#

At noon, I called a contractor.

Asked about mirror repair. Wall repainting. Light fixtures.

He asked when he could visit. I said, "Today."

The soft rebellion had begun.

Not to fix the house — but to **rewrite my presence in it.**

#

That evening, Arjun walked in and paused when he saw the changes.

"You moved everything," he said.

"I did."

"Why?"

"Because I'm here too. And this house forgot that."

#

He didn't reply.

He just walked upstairs.

But I could tell — something had shifted.

And this time, it wasn't the house.

#

That night, Ira showed me her new drawing.

A woman standing on a hill with her arms open wide.

I asked, "Who's this?"

She smiled. "You."

"When a woman stops shrinking, the room either grows with her — or breaks."

The next morning, I set only two plates on the table — one for Ira, one for me.

Arjun came down, saw it, paused.

"You didn't make breakfast for me?"

"No," I said. "I didn't know if you'd be here."

He stood for a moment, like trying to decide whether to be angry or guilty.

He chose silence instead.

He made his own tea.

I didn't feel triumphant.

I felt free.

#

Meera came later, carrying nothing for the first time. No lunchbox. No flowers. Just herself.

She walked in and said, “It’s happening.”

I asked, “What?”

“The house is remembering its softness.”

I smiled.

She cleaned with less movement that day — not slower, just lighter. Like her energy was no longer about scrubbing pain from corners but polishing something brighter.

#

At lunch, I asked her, “Why do you keep showing up?”

“You think I shouldn’t?” she said.

“No. I just… don’t pay you enough to care like this.”

She looked at me for a long time.

Then said, “I’m not here for your money.”

“I know. But then why?”

She walked to the window, looked out at the quiet street.

“Because once, I forgot who I was too.
And someone stayed with me until I remembered.”

#

The contractor arrived later with paint samples and a catalogue.

I chose warm shades. Earth tones. Something that felt like the inside of a heart — soft, steady.

I didn’t ask Arjun’s opinion.

That night, I told him the bedroom wall would be repainted next week.

He stared at me. “So you’re just making all the decisions now?”

I didn’t flinch. “No. I’m finally making mine.”

He didn’t sleep beside me that night.

But I did.

And deeply.

#

The next morning, Ira asked if she could paint too.

I handed her a brush, and we filled a corner of her room with stars.

Tiny white stars on a pale blue wall.

She looked up at me and whispered, “Now the room can

dream too."

I hugged her so tight she squealed.

#

That evening, Meera was in the kitchen when Arjun came home early.

He looked at her — really looked — for the first time since we moved in.

"You're still here?" he asked.

"I always was," she replied.

Something in her tone made him falter.

#

After dinner, he sat across from me and asked, "What are we even doing anymore?"

I said, "We're not doing anything. I am."

"I feel like you've changed."

"I have. I stopped waiting for you to notice me."

He looked down. "I don't know how to fix this."

"I don't need you to fix it," I said. "I need you to face it."

#

He left the table without finishing his tea.

I finished mine.

Slowly. Quietly. Powerfully.

#

Meera placed a jasmine flower on the window that night and turned to me.

"You're not the same woman who moved in here," she said.

"I know."

"And you haven't even started yet."

#

I stood at the mirror again, the one that cracked days ago.

It was still broken.

But I didn't feel the need to replace it.

"Let it stay," I whispered.

"Let it remind me what survived."

CHAPTER 7 – THE BREAKING POINT

"The moment of truth isn't always loud. Sometimes, it comes as a woman who no longer flinches."

I found the photo under the mattress.

It wasn't hidden well. Like most of Arjun's lies — just deep enough that only someone tired of pretending would bother to look.

It was a selfie.

A woman.

A smile that was too familiar.

Naina. The neighbor.

She wore the same scarf she had on the last time we bumped into her at the grocery store.

Arjun's hand was on her shoulder. His wedding ring turned slightly inward.

I didn't scream. Or throw it. Or burn it.

I stared at it for ten minutes, breathing slower with each minute.

Then I folded it and placed it on his pillow.

#

Meera arrived mid-morning.

She didn't ask questions.

But she looked at me with an intensity that felt like a shield.

"You're ready," she said.

"For what?"

"To stop being the one who waits."

#

Arjun came home early that evening.

He saw the photo. Said nothing for a full minute.

Then, "It's not what you think."

I raised my eyebrows. "Then you tell me what it is."

"She needed comfort. We were talking. That's all."

"That's all?"

"Yes," he insisted, too quickly. "Nothing happened."

I nodded. "But something always almost does, doesn't it?"

He sat down, exhausted. Or maybe exposed.

"I've felt invisible, Sanjana. Like you're in your own world."

"And did cheating help you feel seen?"

He winced.

"I didn't cheat," he muttered. "Not really."

"There's no such thing as not really betraying someone."

He looked up at me. And for the first time in months — maybe years — I saw regret that wasn't rehearsed.

"Are you going to leave?" he asked.

"I'm not sure yet," I said. "But I've already started returning to myself."

He hesitated. Then added, voice lower, "I don't know how to fix things. But I've started seeing someone — a counselor. I haven't told you, because I didn't want it to seem like a performance."

I turned to him, genuinely startled.

"You did?"

He nodded.

"I didn't know how to explain why I shut down, or why I kept drifting. But I'm trying to understand it. Not to win you back — just so I don't keep ruining things I care about."

It didn't make the pain disappear.

But it shifted something.

Because it wasn't an excuse.

It was a confession.

#

That night, I made tea for one.
Sat by the window.
The house didn't feel like it was collapsing.
It felt like it was stretching.
Making space.
For me.

#

Meera didn't say much as she wiped the kitchen counters.
But as she left, she turned and said:

"Forgiveness doesn't mean staying.
Sometimes, it means letting go with peace — not punishment."

#

Ira came into the room holding a toy phone.
"Dadda didn't play with me today."
"I know," I said softly.
"Are you mad at him?"
"No, baby."
"Then why do your eyes look like they're full of rain?"

I kissed her forehead.
"Because even flowers need storms sometimes.
Some endings don't explode. They exhale."

#

The next morning, I didn't wait for Arjun to wake up.
I packed a single bag — not to leave him, but to leave the version of myself that kept asking for permission to exist.

Ira sat on the bed watching me fold clothes. Her eyes wide, but not afraid.

"Are we going away?"
"No," I said. "We're staying right here. But I'm going to stay differently now."
"What do you mean?"
"I mean," I smiled, "I'm not going to whisper anymore."

#

Downstairs, Arjun was making coffee.
I placed the bag by the door.

"I'm taking a few days to myself," I said.

He looked startled. "Where are you going?"
"I didn't say I'm leaving the house," I replied. "I'm leaving the version of this life where I pretend you didn't break it."

He opened his mouth. Closed it. Opened it again.
"You can't just emotionally check out."
"I'm not checking out," I said. "I'm checking in. With myself."

#

He followed me into the living room.
"What about us?"
"We'll see," I said. "But for now, I'm not building from broken pieces that you keep dropping."
He threw his arms up. "So that's it? Years together — and this is what it comes down to?"
"No," I said quietly. "This is what it rises up to. A woman who finally sees her own worth."

He stormed out.
The door slammed.
I didn't flinch.

#

Meera came later in the day with fresh flowers.
"Do I still work here?" she asked, almost playfully.
"You don't work here," I said. "You've never been just help. You've been a mirror."
She placed the flowers in a vase. "Then my job is done."
"You're leaving?"
"I'm just... not needed now," she said. "You can see clearly."

I nodded.
But I felt tears behind my eyes.
"Will I forget again?"
"You might," she said gently. "But now you know how to return."

#

That evening, I lit a candle.
No reason. No ceremony. Just a soft flame.

Ira sat beside me and watched it flicker.
"Is it for someone?" she asked.
"Yes," I said. "For me."

#

I picked up the mirror from the guest bathroom. The cracked one.
Carried it outside.
Placed it at the edge of the garden wall.
Then stood and stared at my reflection — broken lines and all.

"I forgive you," I whispered.

"Not for what you endured. But for thinking you had to become smaller to survive it."

#

The wind picked up gently.
Not enough to shake the trees.
But just enough to shift something inside.

That night, I slept deeply.

Not because I was done hurting.
But because I was finally done ignoring the truth.

CHAPTER 8 – THE ROOM WITH THE LOCKED DOOR

*"Some rooms are locked not to keep others out —
but to keep truth from collapsing us too soon."*

The room had always been there.

I had walked past it a hundred times — the narrow door near the back staircase, the one tucked behind the linen closet.

I assumed it was storage.

But I never tried to open it.

Not until now.

#

It was Meera who paused in front of it that day — her hand brushing lightly across the worn brass knob.

"You've never opened this?" she asked.

I shook my head.

"It's time," she said.

"Time for what?"

"To see what you wouldn't have seen before."

#

The key wasn't hard to find. It was taped beneath the drawer in the dining room — as if someone once meant to keep the room closed, but not forever.

My fingers trembled as I turned the lock.

The door creaked open like it had been waiting.

Dust swirled in soft circles as light from the hallway spilled in.

The room was small. Windowless. But not empty.

There was an old armchair. A broken lamp.

A small wooden table covered in a floral cloth.

And on the wall — dozens of Post-it notes, letters, scraps of paper — all taped, pinned, or stuck in place.

Each one written by the same hand.

Aisha's.

#

The handwriting was familiar now. Sharp curves. Slight tilt to the left.

I stepped closer.

Some notes were single words.

"Remember."

"Stay soft."

"Don't flinch."

Others were full confessions.

"I thought love meant staying even when it hurt.
But now I know — that wasn't love. That was fear dressed in compromise."

"He never hit me. But silence can bruise too."

"You're not crazy. You're awake."

#

The more I read, the more I felt like I was reading my own heart.

This wasn't a room.

It was a memory chamber.

A soul trying not to disappear.

#

In the far corner, beneath a cloth-covered box, I found a photograph.

Aisha and Rhea as children.

Smiling. Holding hands.

And on the back:

"To the next woman who thinks she's alone — you're not. I'm still here, in the quiet."

#

I sat on the floor.

For a long time.

No tears. Just breath.

Just... truth.

#

Later that day, Meera returned as I was closing the door again.

"You saw her," she said softly.

"I saw myself."

She nodded, as if that's exactly what she hoped would happen.

#

"You knew about that room?"

"Yes," Meera said. "But it wasn't mine to open."

I leaned against the wall.

"There's so much pain here."

"There's more resilience," she said. "Pain doesn't fill a room like that. Courage does."

"When we transform a space of hiding into a space of healing, we rewrite more than memory — we reclaim it."

That night, after Ira went to sleep and the hallway lights were dim, I opened the locked door again.

But this time, I brought paint.

And a small lamp.

And jasmine oil.

#

I didn't remove Aisha's notes.

I cleaned around them.

Taped the ones peeling off. Aligned the crooked ones gently.

Then I placed a rug in the middle — soft, thick, the kind I used to dream of lying on when I needed to disappear.

I placed a single floor cushion beside the wall.

And in the corner, a small journal, blank.

Waiting.

#

The next morning, Meera stepped into the room and smiled.

"You turned it into a sanctuary," she said.

"No. I think it always was. It just forgot."

Meera nodded. "Like you."

#

We sat there together for ten minutes. No words.

Then she stood and walked to the windowless wall, pressing her hand against it.

"This house is not cursed," she said.

"It's just full of women who thought they had to be small to stay."

"You made it bigger."

#

Ira walked in quietly after Meera left.

She looked around the room, her head tilting like she was trying to listen to something no one had spoken.

"This room feels like a hug," she said.

I laughed — not out of amusement, but release.

"I think it is."

#

That evening, I lit a small candle in the center of the room and sat cross-legged, alone.

I whispered a line I didn't even plan.

"To the women who came before — thank you for surviving long enough to leave a light for me."

And in my mind, I heard the echo of Aisha's words.

"You're not crazy. You're awake."

#

That night, Meera came later than usual.

She didn't clean.

She just walked in, placed a small wooden box on the kitchen counter, and looked at me with softness I hadn't seen in anyone in years.

"This is for you," she said. "But not yet."

"When?"

"When you know you're done needing me."
She turned, walked toward the door.
Paused.
And said:
"I was never here to dust your shelves.
I was here to help you remember who dusts their own soul."
Then she left.

#

I didn't open the box.
Not yet.
I placed it inside the room.
On the table. Beside the journal.
I would open it when I was ready.
And something in me knew —
That time was very, very close.

#

CHAPTER 9 – THE LEAVING LIGHT

"Some people don't stay to be remembered.
They stay until you remember yourself."

The wooden box sat untouched for three days.
Each time I passed it in the small sanctuary room, I felt its weight — not the literal kind, but the kind that asks:
Are you ready to move forward without leaning?
I wasn't sure.

Meera didn't come the next morning.
No knock.
No jasmine.
No soft shuffle of her slippers against the tile.
The house didn't feel empty. It felt… suspended.
As if holding its breath.

By evening, I found a note tucked beneath the cushion in the sanctuary room.
Her handwriting. As familiar now as my own.

"I told you I wasn't here forever.
But I didn't leave.
I just stepped aside — so you could hear your own steps again."

Ira came home from school and asked, "Where's Meera?"
"She's gone for now," I said gently.

"Forever?"
"I don't know."
Ira looked at me, then at the box on the table.
"Maybe she's still watching," she whispered.
I wrapped my arms around her.
"I think she always was."

That night, I opened the box.
Inside was a folded white cloth, embroidered with soft gold stitching. A scarf.
Under it, a single stone — smooth, gray, shaped like a tear. Or a seed.
And beneath that, a piece of paper. One word written on it:
"Begin."

I held the scarf close. It smelled faintly of jasmine and something older — like time itself.
The stone was cool in my hand, grounding.
I didn't cry.
But I wanted to.
Not out of grief — but out of awe.
How had a woman who said so little... left behind so much?

In the corner of the box was something else I hadn't noticed at first — a faded photograph.
Meera, decades younger, standing beside a young girl.
On the back:

"My voice was born the day I lost hers."

I held it for a long time.
She had known pain.
She had known loss.
And still, she showed up in my life like a whisper of grace.
Suddenly, she wasn't magic.
She was memory.
Wound and wisdom.
And somehow, that made her even more sacred.

That evening, I sat with Ira on the front steps.
The sky was burning gold.

"I think Meera was magic," Ira said.

"I think she was memory," I replied.
"What do we do now?"
I smiled, wrapped the scarf around my shoulders.
"Now, we begin."

Letting go is not the end. Sometimes, it's the first time your hands are free to build.

The next day, I repainted the sanctuary room wall by myself.
Soft cream. Barely a shade different than before — but enough for me to know it wasn't the same.
I taped one of Aisha's old notes to the fresh wall.
"Begin."
Below it, I wrote in my own hand:
"But this time, as me."

I spent the afternoon rearranging the shelves.
Boxed old memories. Burned nothing. Buried nothing.
Just... released them.
There's something sacred about sorting through your life without rage.
It means the storm passed.

In the evening, I cooked Ira's favorite dinner — dal and jeera rice with tiny cucumber flowers shaped like stars.
We ate on the floor. No TV. No distractions.
She looked up and asked, "Do you miss Daddy?"
I thought about it.
"Yes," I said. "I miss the version of him I thought he would be."
She nodded like she understood far more than a child should.

That night, I wrote in my journal:

"Meera didn't fix me.
She sat beside me while I remembered how to fix myself.
That's what real love looks like.
That's what I will give my daughter."

Arjun texted me two days later.
"I'm outside. Just want to talk."

I let him in.
He looked tired. Worn. But not angry.

"I'm sorry," he said. "Not just for Naina. For everything."
I nodded. "I know."
"I've started seeing someone... a counselor."
"Good."

He looked around the house — at the new curtains, the clean floors, the walls that felt brighter.
"This doesn't feel like the same place," he said.
"It's not."
He paused. "You look different too."
"I am."

He looked down, then asked, "Is there still a chance?"
I smiled gently.
"There's always a chance.
But I'm not standing in the same place anymore."

He nodded.
Didn't beg. Didn't break.
Just breathed.
And left.

I stood at the door, wrapped in Meera's scarf, watching the light spill across the living room floor like gold water.

"This house is no longer waiting," I whispered.
"It's remembering."

That night, I lit one candle in the sanctuary room.
Not for Meera.
Not for Aisha.
For me.
The version I was still becoming.
The one I would never abandon again

CHAPTER 10 – THE REAL HOME

"Home is not a place. It's the moment you stop asking the world to accept what you already are."

Three months passed.

The jasmine plant Meera had once gifted was now blooming on the front porch, climbing gently up the railing like it knew where it belonged.

I watered it every morning — not out of routine, but reverence.

#

The house had changed.

Not dramatically.

No renovations.

Just warmth.

Lighter curtains.

Softer light bulbs.

Open windows even on cold mornings.

It smelled like ginger tea and floor polish and faint sandalwood.

It smelled like someone had finally made space to exhale.

#

Ira now called the sanctuary room *"Mumma's quiet room."*

Sometimes she came in to color on the floor beside me.

Sometimes she didn't.

But the door was never locked.

That was the difference.

#

One afternoon, I sat down in the sanctuary with my tea and opened the journal Meera left behind — the one that still had so many blank pages.

On the first empty page, I wrote:

"The house is no longer watching me.
I'm watching myself now.
And I am enough."

#

Rhea called one evening.

Just to check in.

She was calm, softer than I remembered.

"I think Aisha would've liked you," she said.

"I think I needed her," I replied.

She paused. "Sometimes we don't meet the people we need. But we meet the echoes they leave behind."

#

The next morning, I helped Ira get ready for her first school play.

She was nervous.

"What if I forget my lines?" she asked.

"Then just smile," I said. "The truth always shows on the face. You can't mess that up."

She smiled.

"Like you do now?"

"Exactly like I do now."

#

That afternoon, after dropping her at school, I stood in the center of the living room.

I looked at the walls. The old photo shelf. The candle Meera left near the window, now half-melted.

And for the first time since we moved in, I said aloud:

"This is my home.

"Wholeness isn't about having everything. It's about no longer needing to be anything else."

One Sunday morning, I left the sanctuary door wide open.

I placed a new journal beside the old one.

A blank page. A clean pen.

A quiet invitation.

Then I left a note near the entry:

"For the next woman who enters this house with questions in her bones and silence in her chest — you are not alone."

#

Later that week, a neighbor — Maya — came by to borrow sugar.

She lingered longer than usual. Eyes scanning the books on my shelf.

"Something feels... peaceful in here," she said.

I smiled. "It didn't always."

She looked at the jasmine on the counter. "You should teach something. Meditation? Writing?"

"I'm not a teacher," I laughed.

But she looked at me differently. "Maybe you're just someone who came back to herself. That's enough."

#

That evening, I lit three candles in the sanctuary room.

One for Aisha.

One for Meera.

One for me.

Ira peeked in and asked, "Can I light one too?"

I handed her the match.

She lit hers and whispered, "This is for all the girls who want to grow up strong."

I didn't correct her.

Because she already understood everything.

#

Arjun called a few days later.

He sounded calmer. Quieter.

"I signed the papers," he said.

I thanked him.

There was no anger. No blame. Just a shared softness — two people who once held each other, now holding space.

"I hope you're happy," he added.

"I am," I said. "And I hope you find that too."

#

The last page of Meera's journal had one final message written in her faint, familiar hand:

"When you no longer need to be watched,
you've finally remembered who's doing the watching."

#

I closed the book.

Took a deep breath.

And for the first time since we moved in —
I wasn't waiting for something to end.
I was living something that had just begun.

* * *

ACKNOWLEDGEMENT

To the version of me who stayed when it would've been easier to leave.

To the One who taught me silence is strength.

To the women who carried me in ways the world didn't see—

my mother, my sisters, and my wife, Ravneet—

thank you for your quiet power and unwavering presence.

To those who didn't ask me to explain my silences—

thank you for letting me write through them.

And to the reader still searching—

I hope this story returns you to yourself.

ABOUT THE AUTHOR

Sukhpreet Singh

writes with silence in his bones and softness in his vision.
He believes stories aren't meant to impress — they're meant to uncover.
He is also the author of Mastering the Art of Customer Care, a practical reflection on empathy, communication, and human connection in professional spaces.
Not Broken, Just Buried is his invitation to anyone who has ever been quietly surviving.
He can be reached at: baapdaada13@gmail.com

BOOKS BY THIS AUTHOR

Mastering The Art Of Customer Care

A practical and insightful look into the world behind the headset — how empathy, clarity, and emotional intelligence shape the customer care experience.

Available now on Kindle.

www.ingramcontent.com/pod-product-compliance
Ingram Content Group UK Ltd.
Pitfield, Milton Keynes, MK11 3LW, UK
UKHW021410190726
13845UKWH00028B/998